PowerKids Readers:

The Bilingual Library of the United States of America™

MONTANA

VANESSA BROWN

TRADUCCIÓN AL ESPAÑOL: MARÍA CRISTINA BRUSCA

The Rosen Publishing Group's
PowerKids Press™ & **Editorial Buenas Letras**™
New York

Published in 2006 by The Rosen Publishing Group, Inc.
29 East 21st Street, New York, NY 10010

First Edition

Book Design: Dean Galiano

Photo Credits: Cover © William Manning/Corbis; p. 5 (flag) © Joseph Sohm; ChromoSohm Inc./Corbis; p. 5 (seal) © 2001 One Mile Up, Incorporated; p. 9 © Richard T. Nowitz/Corbis; p. 11 © Bettmann/Corbis; p. 13 © Corbis; p. 15 © Bettmann/Corbis; p. 17 © Associated Press, AP; p. 19 © Dale C. Spartas/Corbis; p. 21 © Steve Kaufman/Corbis; p. 23 © Lowell Georgia/Corbis; p. 25 © Joel W. Rogers/Corbis; p. 26 © Kennan Ward/Corbis; p. 30 (capital) © Michael Lewis/Corbis; p. 30 (seal) © 2001 One Mile Up, Incorporated; p. 30 (flower) © Darrell Gulin/Corbis; p. 30 (bird) © Darrell Gulin/Corbis; p. 30 (silver and gold) © Walter Urie/Corbis; p. 30 (tree) © Richard Cummins/Corbis; p. 31 (upper left) © Bettmann/Corbis; p. 31 (upper middle) © Associated Press/Wyoming Division of Cultural Resources; p. 31 (upper right) © Associated Press, AP; p. 31 (lower left) © Bettmann/Corbis; p. 31 (lower middle) © Bettmann/Corbis; p. 31 (lower right) © Carole Bellaiche/Sygma/Corbis.

Library of Congress Cataloging-in-Publication Data

Brown, Vanessa, 1963–
Montana / Vanessa Brown ; traducción al español, María Cristina Brusca.— 1st ed.
p. cm. — (The bilingual library of the United States of America) Includes bibliographical references (p.) and index.
ISBN 1-4042-3091-2 (library binding)
1. Montana—Juvenile literature. I. Title. II. Series.
F731.3.B76 2006
978.6—dc22
                                                    2005013784
Manufactured in the United States of America

Due to the changing nature of Internet links, Editorial Buenas Letras has developed an online list of Web sites related to the subject of this book. This site is updated regularly. Please use this link to access the list:

http://www.buenasletraslinks.com/ls/montana

Contents

Contenido

Welcome to Montana

These are the flag and seal of the state of Montana. The state motto is written on the seal. It says *oro y plata*. This is Spanish for "gold and silver." The motto reminds us about the importance of mining to the state.

Bienvenidos a Montana

Estos son la bandera y el escudo de Montana. El lema del estado está escrito en el escudo. El lema dice "oro y plata". Esto nos recuerda la importancia de la minería en el estado.

Montana Flag and State Seal

Bandera y escudo de Montana

Montana Geography

Because of its size, Montana is the fourth-largest state in the United States. Montana borders North Dakota, South Dakota, Wyoming, and Idaho. It also borders the country of Canada.

Geografía de Montana

Por su tamaño, Montana es el cuarto estado de los Estados Unidos. Montana linda con Dakota del Norte, Dakota del Sur, Idaho y Wyoming. También comparte una frontera con el país de Canadá.

CANADA
CANADÁ

Clark Fork River
Río Clark Fork

NORTH DAKOTA
DAKOTA DEL NORTE

Missouri River
Río Misuri

Great Falls

MONTANA

Missoula

Helena

Yellowstone River
Río Yellowstone

Butte

Bozeman

Billings

IDAHO

SOUTH DAKOTA
DAKOTA DEL SUR

WYOMING

Map Key
Claves del mapa

Major City
Ciudad principal

Capital
Capital

River
Río

Map of Montana

Mapa de Montana

Montana has two geographic areas. In the center and the east is the Great Plains region. On the west and southwest are the Rocky Mountains. Montana is known as the Big Sky Country because of its big size and rolling plains.

Montana tiene dos áreas geográficas. En el centro y el este está la región de las Grandes Llanuras. En el oeste y el sudoeste están las Montañas Rocosas. Por su gran tamaño y sus vastas llanuras, Montana es conocido como el País de los Grandes Cielos.

Road Across Montana Plains

Camino en las llanuras de Montana

Montana History

In 1804, explorers Meriwether Lewis and William Clark crossed Montana by the Missouri River. Lewis and Clark's trip opened the western territories to the rest of the United States.

Historia de Montana

En 1804, Los exploradores Meriwether Lewis y William Clark llegaron a Montana a través del Río Misuri. El viaje de Lewis y Clark abrió los territorios del oeste al resto de los Estados Unidos.

Sacagawea Guiding Lewis and Clark

Sacagawea guía a Lewis y Clark

James and Grandville Stuart found gold in Gold Creek, Montana, in 1858. Soon more gold was found in places like Grasshopper Creek and Alder Gulch. Montana's gold brought many people to the state.

James y Grandville Stuart encontraron oro en Gold Creek, Montana, en 1858. Muy pronto, se encontró más oro en otros lugares como Grasshopper Creek y Alder Gulch. El oro de Montana atrajo a mucha gente al estado.

Looking for Gold in Montana

Buscando oro en Montana

In 1876, Indian chief Crazy Horse led 2,000 Dakota and Cheyenne fighters against the U.S. Army. This is known as the Battle of Little Big Horn, one of the most famous battles in America's history.

En 1876, el jefe indio Crazy Horse peleó con 2,000 guerreros dakotas y cheyennes contra el Ejército de E.U.A. Esta lucha es conocida como la Batalla de Little Big Horn y es una de las batallas más famosas de la historia de los Estados Unidos.

The Battle of Little Big Horn

La Batalla de Little Big Horn

Jeannette Rankin was born in Missoula, Montana, in 1880. Rankin was elected to the U.S. Congress in 1916. She became the first woman elected to national office in the United States.

Jeannette Rankin nació en Missoula, Montana, en 1880. Rankin fue elegida para integrar el Congreso de E.U.A., en 1916. Rankin fue la primera mujer en ser elegida para ocupar un cargo nacional en los Estados Unidos.

Jeannette Rankin in Washington, D.C.

Jeannette Rankin en Washington, D.C.

Living in Montana

Montana is a very big place, but fewer than one million people live in the state. There are more animals living in Montana than people. In fact there are three cows for every person in the state.

La vida en Montana

Montana es un lugar muy grande pero menos de un millón de personas viven en el estado. En Montana viven más animales que personas. De hecho, en este estado hay tres vacas por cada habitante.

Cattle in Montana
_____
Ganado en Montana

Native Americans like the Blackfeet, Flathead, Cheyenne, and Dakota have been living in Montana for hundreds of years. Today most of these groups live on reservations. A reservation is an area of land set aside by the goverment.

Grupos de nativos americanos como los Blackfeet, Flathead, Cheyenne y Dakota han vivido en Montana por cientos de años. Hoy, la mayoría de estos grupos vive en reservaciones. Una reservación es una porción de tierra que el gobierno ha destinado a los grupos nativos.

Dancer at a Blackfeet Powwow
—
Danzante en un powwow Blackfeet

Montana Today

Montana attracts many visitors. People from all over the world travel to Montana to enjoy the wildlife. The Glacier National Park is a favorite place for hiking.

Montana, hoy

Montana atrae a muchos visitantes. Personas de todo el mundo viajan a Montana para disfrutar de la vida silvestre. El Parque Nacional Glacier es uno de los lugares favoritos para realizar excursiones.

Hiker in Glacier National Park
_____

Excursionista en el Parque Nacional Glacier

Billings, Great Falls, Missoula, and Butte are important cities in Montana. Helena is the capital of the state.

Billings, Great Falls, Missoula y Butte son ciudades importantes de Montana. Helena es la capital del estado.

Capitol Building in Helena

Capitolio en Helena

Activity: Let's Draw Montana's State Animal

The grizzly bear is Montana's state animal.

Actividad: Dibujemos el animal del estado de Montana

El oso pardo es el animal del estado de Montana.

1

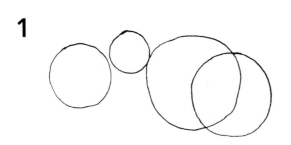

Draw a circle for the head and a smaller circle for the shoulder. Add two more overlapping circles for the belly and rear.

Dibuja un círculo en el lugar de la cabeza y un círculo más pequeño para la espalda. Agrega dos círculos superpuestos para trazar la panza y la parte trasera del oso.

2

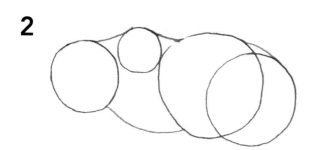

Join the circles with curved lines to make the top of the head and the back. Draw a line below the front circles to form the belly.

Junta los círculos con líneas curvas para trazar la parte de arriba de la cabeza y la espalda. Dibuja una línea por debajo de los círculos delanteros para formar la panza.

3

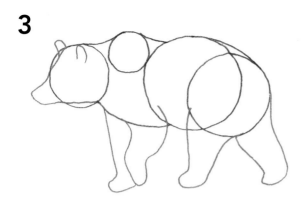

Add the nose and the ears.
Draw the rounded shapes of the
front and rear legs.

Agrega la nariz y las orejas.
Dibuja las formas redondeadas de
las patas delanteras y traseras.

4

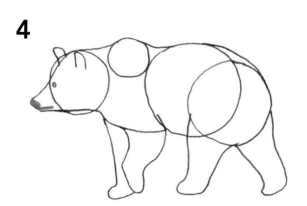

Add the bear's eye, nose, and
mouth.

Agrega el ojo, la nariz y la boca
del oso.

5

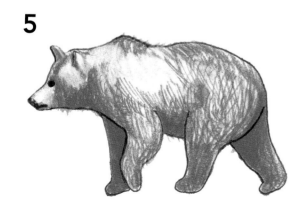

Erase all extra lines. Add shading
and detail to your drawing.

Borra las líneas innecesarias.
Agrega sombras y detalles a tu
dibujo.

Timeline

Cronología

Eastern Montana becomes part of the United States with the Louisiana Purchase.

1803

Con la Compra de Luisiana, Montana oriental pasa a formar parte de los Estados Unidos.

The Lewis and Clark trip enters Montana.

1805

La expedición de Lewis y Clark entra a Montana.

Gold is discovered in Grasshopper Creek.

1862

Se descubre oro en Grasshopper Creek.

General Custer and his troops are defeated in the Battle of Little Big Horn.

1876

El General Custer y sus tropas son vencidos en la Batalla de Little Big Horn.

Montana becomes the forty-first state of the Union.

1889

Montana se convierte en el estado cuarenta y uno de la Unión.

Fort Peck Dam is completed.

1940

Se termina la represa Fort Peck.

A new state constitution takes effect.

1973

Entra en vigencia la nueva constitución del estado.

Theodore Kaczynski, known as the Unabomber, is captured in Lincoln, Montana.

1996

Theodore Kaczynski, conocido como el Unabomber, es capturado en Lincoln, Montana.

Montana Events

February
"Race to the Sky" Sled Dog Race
from Helena to Seeley Lake
Winter Carnival in Whitefish

May
Cherry Blossom Festival in Polson

June
Governor's Cup Marathon
in Helena
Music Festival in Red Lodge

July
Home of Champions Rodeo in
Red Lodge
North American Indian Days
in Browning

August
Festival of Nations in Red Lodge
Western Montana Fair and
Rodeo in Missoula

October
Bison Roundup near Moiese

November
Bald Eagle Gathering near Helena

December
Christmas Stroll in Bozeman

Eventos en Montana

Febrero
Carrera de trineos "Carrera al Cielo", desde
Helena hasta Lago Seeley
Festival de invierno, en Whitefish

Mayo
Festival del pimpollo de la cereza, en Polson

Junio
Maratón Copa del Gobernador,
en Helena
Festival de música, en Red Lodge

Julio
Rodeo Hogar de los Campeones,
en Red Lodge
Días de los Indios Norteamericanos,
en Browning

Agosto
Festival de las naciones, en Red Lodge
Feria y rodeo de Montana Occidental,
en Missoula

Octubre
Rodeo de bisontes, cerca de Moiese

Noviembre
Reunión Bald Eagle, cerca de Helena

Diciembre
Paseos de Navidad, en Bozeman

Montana Facts/Datos sobre Montana

Population
902,000

Población
902,000

Capital
Helena

Capital
Helena

State Motto
Oro y Plata

Lema del estado
Oro y plata

State Flower
Bitterroot

Flor del estado
Verdolaga de Montana

State Bird
Western Meadowlark

Ave del estado
Pradero occidental

State Nickname
The Treasure State/
Big Sky Country

Mote del estado
El Estado del Tesoro/
País de los Grandes Cielos

State Tree
Ponderosa Pine

Árbol del estado
Pino Ponderosa

State Song
"Montana"

Canción del estado
"Montana"

Famous Montanans/Montaneses famosos

Sacagawea
(1786?—1812?)

Indian guide
Guía indígena

Washakie
(1804?—1900)

Indian chief
Jefe indio

Jeannette Rankin
(1880–1973)

Politician
Política

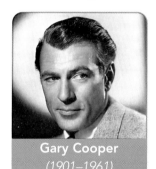

Gary Cooper
(1901–1961)

Actor
Actor

Myrna Loy
(1905–1993)

Actor
Actriz

David Lynch
(1946–)

Writer / Film director
Escritor/ Director de cine

Words to Know/Palabras que debes saber

battle
batalla

border
frontera

mining
minería

reservation
reservación

31

Here are more books to read about Montana:
Otros libros que puedes leer sobre Montana:

In English/En inglés:

Montana
Hello U.S.A
by Ladoux, Rita
Lerner Publications; 2nd Rev&Ex
edition (November 1, 2002)

Montana
Rookie Read-About Geography
by Trumbauer, Lisa
Children's Press, 2004

Words in English: 364

Palabras en español: 383

Index

Índice